Archie Appleby

the terrible case
of the creeps

Archie Appleby The Terrible Case of the Creeps

Text © Kaye Baillie
Illustrations © Krista Brennan

Published by Wombat Books 2017
www.wombatbooks.com.au
PO Box 1519,
Capalaba QLD 4157
Australia

National Library of Australia Cataloguing-in-Publication entry

Creator: Baillie, Kaye, author.
Title: Archie Appleby : the terrible case of the creeps /
Kaye Baillie; illustrated by Krista Brennan.
ISBN: 9781925563016 (paperback)
Target Audience: For primary school age.
Subjects: Children's stories.
Other Creators/Contributors:
 Brennan, Krista, illustrator.

Wombat Books
Stories you'll want to share

Archie Appleby

the terrible case
of the creeps

kaye
baillie

Illustrated by krista brennan

For my sister, Janny.
Miss you. x

chapter one

'You're staying at Aunt Ruth's and that's that,' said Mum.

'Not Aunt Ruth's,' Archie groaned.

Mum closed her suitcase. 'Go and pack your bag.'

'Why can't I stay at Josh's house?'

'I told you. He's going away. Besides, I've asked Aunt Ruth. Her house is right on the way.'

'I bet she doesn't really want me to stay.' Archie followed his mother to the lounge.

'She did take a little convincing,' Mum said, looking thoughtful. 'But I told her you'd be good company with Uncle Jock away and that you'd help her in the garden.'

Archie thought about his last visit to his great aunt's—so many boring lectures on herb growing; not to mention hours and hours of weeding. Then she'd force him to handpick every single snail from the garden. If that wasn't bad enough, Aunt Ruth always served up brown sloppy stew while she blabbed on about the *good old days.*

But worst of all, she had a basement—a dark, scary basement. It gave Archie the creeps. Whatever was down there was a mystery. And Archie planned to keep it that way. 'I bet Uncle Jock's not on a holiday.'

'Where else would he be?' said Mum.

'Locked in the basement, of course.'

'Archie! Don't make up silly stories. Every time you do that, something happens— something that causes *a lot* of trouble.'

Archie rolled his eyes. All he ever did was tell the truth. It wasn't his fault if no one ever believed him. Last year he'd been convinced that his maths teacher was trying to hypnotise him and turn him into a slave. The school had called his parents after the teacher reported being locked out of the classroom. Archie received a good talking to and plenty of after school chores. It had all been totally unfair.

His mother continued. 'Do you really want to come all the way to Cousin Cecil's funeral? You won't like it and I don't think I could stand all the whinging. Besides, you hardly knew Cecil.'

Archie thought about it—two nights with just him and Aunt Ruth in her creepy old house. And what about her mangy, three-legged dog, Bob, with the bung eye? Aunt Ruth always let Bob eat at the table, even though he slobbered.

On the other hand, if Archie went to the funeral, he would have to suffer a four hour car trip with his parents, where his dad would play country western music all the way. The day

after that would be his dad's cousin's funeral—
Archie had never been to one of those and
never wanted to. Then the next day would be
another four hour trip home.

'Alright. I'll go to Aunt Ruth's.' *With any
luck, Uncle Jock might come back.*

chapter two

Archie checked his bag: football, comics, torch, Gooey Gum. 'Right. Packed.'

Archie re-read the note he'd written.

If I disappear it means Aunt Ruth has locked me in her basement. Send the police and maybe an ambulance. Her address is 13 Black Road, Shadowville.

Archie Appleby.

Archie put the note in an envelope marked, *How to find Archie,* and placed it on his pillow.

'Ready?' asked Dad. 'What's that?'

'If you and Mum get stuck somewhere,

people need to know where to find me.'

'You'll be back home before you know it,' said Dad.

Hopefully. Archie tapped his nose three times for luck.

***

Later that morning, Archie and his parents drove into the country. When Archie saw the Welcome to Shadowville sign, he knew they were almost at Aunt Ruth's turnoff.

If only they would get a flat tyre. He heard Dad put on the indicator as they turned into Black Road. They passed Mr Cronk's place. He'd lived there for as long as Archie could remember, and Aunt Ruth always talked about him like they were best buddies. Above the trees, Archie saw Aunt Ruth's house with its huge rooftop and chimneys. He sank down as Dad drove through the gate.

'Here we are,' said Mum in a cheery voice.

Archie didn't feel too cheery. He was starting to think he'd made the wrong choice. 'When will Uncle Jock be back?' said Archie, peering out the window. 'He's *actually* fun.'

'It's a bit of a mystery, really,' said Dad, hopping out of the car. 'Aunt Ruth said he went on an overdue holiday a week ago. She didn't say where.'

'Gee, that's a long time to spend in the basement,' joked Archie. *Though, could he be …?*

'Oh, shush, Archie. You're not going to turn this into another one of your ridiculous imaginings,' said Mum, yanking open Archie's door. 'Out you hop.'

Archie was frogmarched to the front door and Dad pushed the doorbell.

Glark-glark! Glark-glark! It sounded like a warning cry from an old crow.

Archie looked around at the garden. The fish pond was full of green slime. 'How gross,' he said.

Giant wind chimes hung on a rotting tree branch. They swung in the breeze, clanging deeply like a church bell. Then, Archie looked at the rows of gloomy windows.

'I've … changed my mind. I think I'll go to the funeral instead.'

'You can't back out now,' said Mum.

'Yes I can,' said Archie. 'Just say I'm going with you.'

'Yoo hoo! I'm in the garden,' came Aunt Ruth's voice.

'Come on,' said Mum. 'I'm sure it won't be that bad.'

Archie dragged his feet as he followed Mum and Dad to where Aunt Ruth was pulling out some weedy-looking stuff. She shoved it in a bucket and wiped her hands on her apron. Her eyes met Archie's from behind a long beaky nose.

Archie was sure now he'd made the wrong choice.

chapter three

'Hello, Aunt Ruth,' said Mum, giving her a hug.

'Hello, Ruth,' said Dad. He kind of shook her hand.

Archie stood behind his parents, wondering if Aunt Ruth had shrunk since he last saw her.

Aunt Ruth blinked quickly and twitched her mouth. She wore two cardigans with buttons in the wrong holes, a brown woollen skirt and moccasins. Her long white hair looked as though she'd been through a storm and worse were the black tufts sprouting from her legs.

'What took you so long?' said Aunt Ruth.

'Sorry about that,' said Dad. 'There's always a bit to do before we go somewhere.'

'Balderdash,' said Aunt Ruth. 'Punctuality is a virtue.'

Archie brushed his shoe over the gravelly path.

'Well, well. I'll have young Archie all to myself, will I?' said Aunt Ruth with a grin.

'Say hello,' said Mum, giving Archie a poke.

'Hi.'

'Don't just stand there,' Aunt Ruth said, looking Archie up and down. 'Make yourself useful and carry that bucket for me.'

Archie slowly lifted the bucket and followed Aunt Ruth inside. 'The house is just as I remember,' he said. 'Creepy.'

Aunt Ruth narrowed her eyes.

Dad made a face at Archie as if to say, *watch out*!

'Tea, everyone?' said Aunt Ruth.

'Yeah, they would love tea,' said Archie quickly. He didn't want his parents to leave him alone with Aunt Ruth too soon.

They went through to what Aunt Ruth called the grand dining room. The table was like something from the medieval days. Archie could see it seating a hundred people. There were a tea set and biscuits at one end, so Archie decided to sit way down the other end—the furthest he could get from Aunt Ruth and her horrible cooking.

Aunt Ruth poured Dad's tea. 'Sorry to hear about your cousin but Cecil was a rotten old fuddy-duddy. The last time I saw him he said I was crazy. He called me a witch! I don't like that kind of talk and I never forget. Still, I suppose it wasn't nice, you know, the way he died.'

'Yeah, how did he die?' said Archie. 'Nobody's told me.'

Mum and Dad looked at each other.

Aunt Ruth shuffled over next to Archie and leaned in close to his ear. 'It seems he was poisoned—very strange. Biscuit?'

He slid a biscuit off the plate with his finger. 'Thanks.'

'Oh, dear. I've forgotten the sugar.' Aunt Ruth put the plate down and shuffled off.

Archie sniffed the biscuit. 'Was Cecil really poisoned? How come you never told me?'

'Because it sounds horrible,' said Mum.

'He ate some kind of rare plant,' said Dad, wincing. 'Terrible way to go.'

Archie shuddered. 'Aunt Ruth probably sent Cecil one of her plants—she grows all kinds of weird stuff.'

Aunt Ruth came out of the kitchen.

'She didn't even look sorry about Cecil,' whispered Archie. 'Are you sure you want to leave me here?'

'Behave yourself,' Mum whispered back.

Bob jumped up on a chair so Archie snuck him his biscuit. There were soon slobbery crumbs everywhere.

'Did you just give Bob your biscuit?' screeched Aunt Ruth.

'He looked hungry,' said Archie.

'There's chocolate in those. Chocolate is like poison to a dog. Didn't you know that?'

'You seem to know a lot about poison,' said Archie suspiciously. 'Maybe Cecil ate one of your chocolate biscuits.'

'He wasn't a dog, you silly boy!' Aunt Ruth's face twitched. 'I see you're going to need some of my special attention the next few days. I'll soon sort you out.'

A little while later, Archie stood at the front of the house and watched his parents' car grow smaller as it crept down the long driveway. It blinked, then disappeared.

See you later—I hope.

chapter four

Aunt Ruth bustled Archie back inside. Just like in one of those scary movies he didn't like to watch, the big, old door creaked and groaned as Aunt Ruth closed it with a thud.

'Come with us, Archie. We'll take you to your room.'

Archie grabbed his bag. 'It's okay. I can find it myself.'

'Nonsense. We can chat on the way.'

Bob went first, hobbling down the lengthy hall. All kinds of paintings and photos filled the walls. Aunt Ruth stopped at each one.

'This is me with my mother when I was a little girl ...'

'This is me with Bob when he had four legs ...'

'This one was taken just as Bob got too close to ... um ... er ... a crocodile ...'

'A crocodile.' Archie shivered, then moved on. 'What about this one? Is it a fancy dress party?'

'That's our wedding photo,' snapped Aunt Ruth.

Archie choked trying not to laugh. He thought Uncle Jock looked like a clown in his yellow suit and with his red bulbous nose. 'So when is Uncle Jock coming back? He is coming back, isn't he?'

Aunt Ruth raised her eyebrows. 'I'm sure in time he'll show up. One way or another.'

'Is he lost?' asked Archie.

'What a nosy young chap you are,' she said. 'Move along now.'

Archie did as he was told until they finally

got to the end of the hall.

'You remember this room, don't you, Archie?'

'Yeah. The one next to the basement stairs.' Archie peered over the handrail and into the blackness below. It looked deeper and darker than he remembered, and he was sure he could hear something—or someone—groaning.

'Stay away from the basement, won't you?' said Aunt Ruth. 'I don't want you going missing.'

Archie felt queasy. He didn't like the idea of going missing. He didn't like the idea of being at Aunt Ruth's—full stop.

chapter five

Archie poked his head inside the bedroom. 'Err, does it have the same bed? Last time it was really hard.'

'I can see I'm going to have to toughen you up, young man. In you go,' she said, prodding him with her bony finger.

The room had a wall of shelves filled with hundreds of books and ornaments. Newspaper and rubbish bulged from the old fireplace, and hanging above it was a huge painting of Aunt Ruth. Archie wondered how he could possibly sleep in there, especially with her beady eyes staring down on him.

'When you've unpacked, you can help in the kitchen. The potatoes need peeling. Come on, Bob.'

Archie listened at the door until Aunt Ruth's footsteps disappeared. Then he rummaged through his bag, took out the Gooey Gum and plugged up the keyhole. 'There, that should do it.' When he turned round, Aunt Ruth's creepy stare made him jump.

'Aaahh!' Archie grabbed an old broom from the corner and hoisted up a spare bed sheet. He managed to drape it over Aunt Ruth's portrait. What a relief! He unpacked, then crept back up the dark hall, checking behind him all the way to the kitchen.

'Do you think we could leave the hall light on?' said Archie.

'No. I'm not made of money.' Aunt Ruth plonked a large bowl of potatoes on the table. 'Aren't they beautiful? Food from the earth— straight from my veggie garden. You get peeling and I'll get chopping. Then we'll put in the meat, carrots and some of my special herbs. I like to make a double batch. You never know who might need feeding.'

Who else was Aunt Ruth expecting?

'What kind of special herbs?' asked Archie, thinking about Cecil.

'You'll see. Then while the stew is cooking, we'll have a walk round the garden. I'm quite proud of some of my hybrid plants—I seem to have a talent for creating new species.'

Snarl! Bob raised his hackles at her last words.

'Stop it, Bob. Don't be like that.'

'What's wrong with him?' asked Archie.

Aunt Ruth's mouth twitched. 'As I was saying, we'll go for a walk. After that I'd like you to have a bath and be seated at the table for dinner at six o'clock sharp.'

'Bath? What about a shower?'

'You'll have a bath,' snapped Aunt Ruth.

'I'll bring my footy when we go outside. There's plenty of room for a kick.'

'No you won't. You'll pay attention and learn something about gardening and the use of ancient herbs. The potatoes aren't going to peel themselves, you know.'

Archie imagined his dad's country western music. Somehow it didn't seem so bad now.

***

As they walked round the yard, Aunt Ruth urged Archie to look at every plant—dead or alive. 'Isn't my veggie patch wonderful? Dig up a few more carrots, would you, Archie. And after that you can give those plants some water.'

Archie stuck the fork into the dirt and pulled up some gnarled carrots, then plonked them in a bucket. He grabbed the hose and watered the strange spiky-looking plants.

'Good. We can use the carrots tomorrow,' said Aunt Ruth.

Archie rolled his eyes. All this food wasn't just for the two of them. Aunt Ruth was definitely feeding someone else.

'Now, this is where I grow my herbs,' said Aunt Ruth, as they moved to the next garden bed.

'What kind are they?'

'Sage, parsley and rosemary.'

'What about these weird looking ones? They look like weeds.'

'That's horny wolf weed and that's devil's beard,' she said.

Archie made a face. 'You didn't put those in the stew, did you?'

'Not today. But I did use eye of newt.'

'Eye of newt! You mean that stuff is real?'

'Oh, it's very real,' Aunt Ruth said with a grin.

'Blaahh,' said Archie. He could just see her stirring that eye of newt in a big black pot.

chapter six

After listening to Aunt Ruth go on and on about her plants and how everyone should love gardening, Archie was relieved to be alone in his bedroom. He looked at his watch—5.30pm. Bath time. He turned on the squeaky, old taps. Archie hadn't had a bath since he was seven. When the bath was deep enough, he hopped in with one of his comics.

Before long there was a loud knock at his door.

'Who's there?' Archie called.

'Aunt Ruth, of course! I told you six o'clock.'

'I'll just finish this page,' he called again.

'What's this!' yelled Aunt Ruth.

Archie hurried out of the bath with his towel on. He cringed when he saw Aunt Ruth pointing at the sheet above the fireplace. He needed to think quick. 'I was doing some interior decorating.'

'I see,' said Aunt Ruth with a scowl. 'I could do without your decorating ideas. Thankfully you're only here two nights. Perhaps we should make it one.'

Archie gulped. 'Guess I'd better get ready then.'

In the dining room, Archie peered into a steaming pot full of gluggy stew. But even worse was the pot of boiled eggs right next to it. He hated eggs! Eggs were the smelliest, most revolting things ever.

Bob snuffled loudly in the corner, then yelped and ran round barking.

'What's he doing?' said Archie.

'Just a rat,' said Aunt Ruth. 'Don't worry.

Bob will deal with it.'

Sure enough, Bob chased the rat out through the door to the garden. What next? Bats, giant spiders and a snake or two? This was the strangest place ever. Archie was beginning to wonder if he'd even make it through the night.

Bob came back and sat up at the table.

'Perhaps we can eat now,' said Aunt Ruth. She plonked a ladle full of stew on Archie's plate. Then she spooned an egg from the pot.

Archie shook his head and waved his hands. 'Nooo!'

It was too late. He stared at the shiny, rubbery white egg on top of his stew. Pinching his nose, Archie tossed the egg back into the pot. 'If you eat eggs, I'll have to sit down the end of the table. The smell makes me sick.'

Archie quickly realised that Aunt Ruth had turned a strange shade of purple.

'How odd,' she said. 'But now there's more for me.' She stuck her fork into an egg, shoving the whole thing in her mouth.

Archie lost his appetite. He ate as little as he could, then finally pushed away his plate. 'I don't feel so well. I think it was that eye of newt. Can I watch telly now, please?'

'I don't think so. After you've cleared the table, we'll do a nice jigsaw together.'

Jigsaw!

Aunt Ruth tilted her head. 'Don't look so worried, Archie. Jigsaws are fun.'

A little later, Archie reluctantly followed Aunt Ruth into the lounge room. She tipped the jigsaw pieces onto the table.

'What's it called?' asked Archie. 'Wolf Man?' He looked at the pictures on the lid and saw an old shack, bats and a full moon. But the worst part was the Wolf Man howling at the moon. 'Are you sure you want to do this puzzle?'

'Jock never liked this jigsaw either. But I like it. Nothing like a bit of scary stuff now and then,' she laughed. 'Especially on a stormy night like tonight.'

Scary. Aunt Ruth was managing that all by herself.

They began doing the jigsaw, piece by piece. The creepy image of the Wolf Man came together. Its evil yellow eyes burned right into Archie's. He saw the creature move towards him, opened mouth slavering, teeth bared …

Suddenly Archie saw a bright flash of lightning outside, followed by a booming crash of thunder. He half expected the Wolf Man to burst through the door along with a dozen bats. Rain pelted down while the wind and trees scratched at the windows.

Glark-glark! Glark-glark! went the doorbell.

Archie wanted to dive under the table.

'Now who could that be?' said Aunt Ruth. She shuffled towards the door.

'Don't open it,' yelled Archie. 'It's the Wolf Man!'

chapter seven

Aunt Ruth slowly opened the door. A burst of rain flicked inside.

Archie gulped when he saw a shadowy shape at the doorway.

'What are you doing here on a night like this?' said Aunt Ruth. 'Come in, come in.'

The shape, with its huge hat and dripping coat, came inside. 'Sorry, Ruth. I seem to have made a big puddle on your floor. Thought I'd check that you had no leaks or what not. And with Jock gone, thought you might need an extra hand.' A man took off his hat and whacked it on his waterproof pants.

Aunt Ruth glanced quickly at Archie, then back to the man. 'We already talked today about what needs doing,' she said in a hushed voice. 'And we haven't got any leaks or trouble.'

Archie cleared his throat, then sniffed.

Aunt Ruth closed the door. 'How rude of me. This is my great-nephew, Archie.'

'Hello, young fella. I'm Harold Cronk from up the road. Remember me? Heard you were visiting.'

'What did you mean, "with Uncle Jock gone?" Do you know where he is?'

'No, I don't, young fella. Seems he's disappeared.'

Archie thought Mr Cronk looked a bit shifty. He didn't trust him. Not one bit.

'Have you eaten, Harold? There's plenty of stew left over. Archie eats like a bird,' said Aunt Ruth.

'No need. I'm right. Your Aunt Ruth's one heck of a cook, isn't she?' Mr Cronk said to Archie.

Aunt Ruth looked pleased and playfully slapped Mr Cronk on the shoulder. 'Nice of you to say, Harold. Jock never says a kind word about my cooking.'

Mr Cronk chuckled. 'You can cook for me any time, Ruth. I bet you don't miss Jock's complaining.'

Aunt Ruth turned to Archie. 'If it's not Jock complaining, it's Archie. Don't know what I'm going to do with him. He even covered my portrait in the guest bedroom with a sheet!'

'We'll soon have him sorted out, hey, Ruth?' Mr Cronk chuckled. 'Anyhow, I'll head home now. Seems you two are alright. We'll talk tomorrow about … finishing things off.'

Finishing things off! And what did Mr Cronk mean by *sorting him out*?

After Mr Cronk left and Aunt Ruth had mopped the wet floor, she announced it was bedtime.

Archie hesitated. He thought about the

long, dark passage. He thought about being in that big, old room by himself. He thought about Aunt Ruth and Mr Cronk and their evil plans. 'Can I stay up a bit longer?'

'No.'

'I'm thirsty. Can I have a glass of water?'

'Scoot!' Aunt Ruth snapped.

'Alright. Night.' Archie zipped down the passage into his room and slammed the door. He didn't like the room's musty smell. Why hadn't he noticed the big cracks on the walls before? And why did the windows have a foggy glaze? Even the single dusty light globe, swaying on its long cord, flickered as though it was about to go out. Archie put his torch under his pillow, then wedged a chair under the doorknob. He got ready for bed, then jumped in with a comic, pulling the heavy, old blankets up to his nose.

After a while, Archie drifted off to sleep.

Tap, tap, tap. What was that noise? Archie

groggily hopped out of bed and put his ear to the floor. He heard it again. *Tap, tap, tap,* followed by horrible sounds. *Hisssss. Hisssss. Hisssss.* He was wide awake now.

Archie shifted the chair from his door and peeped outside. The lights were still on in the dining room. When he heard the basement stairs creaking he ducked back inside. His heart

pounded when he saw Aunt Ruth coming up from the basement, carrying an empty plate and the herb bucket.

'I knew it,' he whispered. 'She's feeding Uncle Jock.'

Archie gently closed his door, put the chair back and jumped into bed. He knew he was right about Uncle Jock. Tomorrow he would rescue him. Tomorrow, he would go down into the deep, dark basement.

chapter eight

The next morning there was a loud knock on Archie's door. 'Who is it?' he mumbled.

'Aunt Ruth, of course. Rise and shine. It's time for porridge.'

Archie dragged himself out of bed. He'd hardly slept a wink with the rain, thunder and lightning. Then there was the tapping and the horrible hissing sounds from the basement.

'How's the porridge?' asked Aunt Ruth. 'Here, have some more. It's good for you,' she said, standing ready with a ladle full.

'No, thanks,' said Archie, putting his hand over his bowl.

'Righto, well here's the plan for today. We'll do the dishes, then head straight out to the garden. There's pruning and de-snailing to be done.'

Archie pushed his bowl aside. 'I heard weird tapping sounds coming from underneath my room last night. What would that be?'

Aunt Ruth spun round. 'Tapping. Hmmm. Well, I don't know.'

'The basement's right under my room, isn't it?' said Archie.

'Yes. Must be rats, I suppose. Bob does his best to keep the numbers down.'

'I heard hissing sounds too. Are there snakes down there as well?'

Aunt Ruth snorted. 'It's nothing to worry about, Archie. Might be a burst pipe.'

Archie stood up. 'That sounds serious. Let's go take a look.'

'To the garden!' ordered Aunt Ruth.

Archie pushed the wheelbarrow to an

overgrown section of the garden.

'We're going to tidy this up,' said Aunt Ruth. 'Over there, Harold has started preparing my new greenhouse. And Jock can't stop me this time! He's never appreciated my gardening skills. I'm going to display my incredible creation and invite horticultural experts to see what I've done. I'll be famous!'

Famous, alright, when the police get hold of you.

'Morning, you two,' called Mr Cronk. 'I've brought back the shears I borrowed from Jock way back. Reckon we'll be needing them for this job,' he chuckled.

Mr Cronk and Aunt Ruth walked off to a secluded part of the garden and began whispering. Archie decided now was the perfect time to check out the basement.

He scurried inside, down the hall and stood at the top of the basement stairs. He tried the light but it didn't work, so he ran to his room and fetched his torch. Down, down, down the stairs he went, until he came to the door at the bottom. He turned the rusted doorknob slowly …

'ARCHIE! Is that you down there?'

Archie's heart jumped. He looked up to see Aunt Ruth at the top of the stairs with Bob beside her, barking like mad. 'What are you doing? I left you pruning.'

'I … I … got bored and thought I'd go for a walk. Then I dropped my, umm, torch down these stairs. Luckily it still works … see.' He shone the torch in Aunt Ruth's face.

'Put that away. I don't want to see you anywhere near the basement again. Do you hear me?'

'Yes, Aunt Ruth.'

chapter nine

Archie was exhausted from pruning, chopping and raking. He'd also filled one bucket with snails. Now he knew why Aunt Ruth wanted him to stay: to be her slave. Wait until he told his parents about this. They'd never let him stay at Aunt Ruth's again.

'You've earned lunch,' said Aunt Ruth. 'Put those tools away, then wash up. I've made sandwiches.'

As Archie put the

wheelbarrow and tools back in the shed, he saw Aunt Ruth with Mr Cronk by the greenhouse. He wasn't going to waste another chance to find Uncle Jock.

He ran inside, fetched his torch and zipped down the basement steps. He tried the door but it was stuck!

Hisssss. Hisssss. Hisssss. BANG! BANG! Those sounds were coming from inside the basement alright.

He hammered on the door. 'Uncle Jock! I've come to save you.'

'Yoo hoo, Archie. Lunch is ready,' called Aunt Ruth.

'Blast it,' muttered Archie. He leapt up the steps two at a time. When he reached the top, Aunt Ruth was waiting.

'Again! What

were you doing down there this time?' she shouted.

'Er, nothing. I just wanted to make sure there wasn't a flood, you know, from the pipe.'

'There are big rats down there, Archie. They munch and crunch on boys like you. If you know what's good for you, you'll stay away.' Aunt Ruth stood so close to Archie, he could see her nose hairs.

Archie knew he'd better follow Aunt Ruth to the dining room. Mr Cronk was waiting there with Bob.

'Ruth was good enough to ask me to stay for lunch,' said Mr Cronk.

'That's handy,' said Archie. 'You'll be able to check the burst pipe.'

'What burst pipe? I thought we were going to talk about the finishing touches on the greenhouse—you know, for Roxy.'

Aunt Ruth kicked Mr Cronk under the table. 'There was no burst pipe, Archie. Just the wind.'

'Really? And who's this Roxy?' said Archie.

'Eat up, Archie,' said Aunt Ruth. 'I'm sure you'll like my garden salad sandwiches.'

This could be my last meal, thought Archie. *If I uncover what's really going on, things are going to get bad.*

Only Bob's stomach gurgled and plopped to break the silence.

chapter ten

Archie didn't get a chance for the rest of the day to rescue Uncle Jock. Aunt Ruth had him weeding, harvesting and planting seeds to grow another weird herb—lungwort.

'Yes, Archie, lungwort. It helps to heal cuts,' she said, handing him the seeds.

Archie thought she was probably going to poison him. Just like Cousin Cecil. Just like she was probably doing to Uncle Jock! There was no way he was going to eat any lungwort.

Aunt Ruth was never far away. She even walked Archie to his bedroom when it was time for his bath. Then, when he came out, Aunt

Ruth and Bob just happened to be standing there. 'Oh, good. All nice and clean for dinner,' said Aunt Ruth.

Archie forced a smile.

Dinner was stew again, except luckily there were no eggs. Dessert was some kind of lemon gloop. Archie knew better this time and didn't say a word about the food.

'Your parents called. They'll be here in the morning. Then you'll be off home,' said Aunt Ruth.

Archie could see she looked pleased, and he felt relieved to think about leaving. But what about finding Uncle Jock? 'I was really hoping to see Uncle Jock. When's he coming back?'

'That all depends on whether he comes back, doesn't it? And who knows when that will be.' Aunt Ruth's mouth tightened and twitched from side to side.

Archie wasn't going to let Aunt Ruth get away with this. He would sort things out, tonight.

That night, when Archie was safely in bed, he made a plan. He would wait until Aunt Ruth was fast asleep, then free Uncle Jock once and for all. He shuddered at the thought of going to the basement in the middle of the night. But it had to be done.

Archie struggled to stay awake, and before long, he drifted off to sleep.

Tap, tap, tap. Archie opened his eyes and looked at his watch. It was five o'clock in the morning. He threw on his clothes, grabbed his torch, then snuck into the hall. Everything was quiet. He took a deep breath and started down the stairs. Round and round Archie crept until he reached the bottom. He turned the doorknob and pushed. The door opened. *Creak!* He shone his torch inside. Something scuttled along the floor. Rats! There were old boxes, suitcases, shelves and even car parts.

Tap, tap, tap.

'Uncle Jock. Are you in here? Uncle Jock. It's me, Archie. I've come to save you.'

Archie waved his torch this way and that way. There was no sign of Uncle Jock, only spiders' webs and junk galore. Then he spied something—a track through the dust on the floor. He followed it to a door on the other side of the room.

Archie took hold of the doorknob. It felt hot. He tapped his nose three times, then slowly... turned ... the doorknob.

chapter eleven

Blazing hot light shot out. Archie flung his arm up to cover his eyes. He heard a loud droning sound. *HUMM! HUMM! HUMM!* Something lashed out, wildly swishing. Archie stumbled backwards as he tried to get away from the long, prickly green arms. This thing had gigantic mouths, opening and closing, hissing and snapping.

HISSSSS! HISSSSS! HISSSSS!

'Aaaahh!!' Archie ran for his life—straight into Aunt Ruth!

'I warned you not to come in here, Archie. Now look what you've done. You've upset my Roxanne.'

'What is it?' yelled Archie. 'Did it eat Uncle Jock?'

Aunt Ruth gave Archie a stony look.

Bob raced in and burst out barking.

HISSSSS! HISSSSS! HISSSSS! BANG! BANG!

'Roxy is upset. And she's very, very hungry.'

'Did that thing eat Bob's leg? Is that what happened? And it probably ate Uncle Jock and now you want it to eat me!'

'Come here, Archie,' said Aunt Ruth reaching for him.

'Help! Help!'

chapter twelve

'Somebody help!!' screamed Archie.

'Would you calm down,' said Aunt Ruth. 'You've done nothing but complain since you got here and I've had enough! It's time I set you straight. I knew if you saw my Roxanne, you'd freak out and now I'm going to make sure you don't tell anyone about her!'

'Help!' screamed Archie.

'There there, Roxy, there there.' Aunt Ruth crooned to the giant thrashing plant like it was a baby. She put some leftover stew and some large moths inside the door, then closed it. The hissing and banging stopped.

Archie leaned against the wall, sweat dripping from his brow. 'What is that thing?'

'A Venus Flytrap Gigantus,' said Aunt Ruth, looking proud of herself.

'A what?' said Archie, slowly inching away.

'My hybrid wonder plant—my incredible creation. She came to me by accident. I was experimenting, crossing and grafting different plants, trying to make one that would eat flies and pests. Roxanne was the result. She kept growing and growing and growing. I used to have her on the kitchen sill until she outgrew the pot. Then I put her in a bigger pot in the lounge—she outgrew that too. Jock said she'd have to go. And I said that he'd have to go! I put her down here just until her new greenhouse is built and then, and only then, will she be revealed to the world! Not by a nosy boy like you. She's going to make scientific and horticultural history! And with Jock gone, I can get on with it.'

'Did Roxanne eat Uncle Jock? Did she?!'

chapter thirteen

Aunt Ruth looked a strange shade of purple again.

'First Bob's leg, then Uncle Jock and now me!' Archie raced up the stairs and into his room. He dragged every bit of furniture across the floor and piled it in front of the door.

Knock.   Knock.

Knock. 'Archie.'

'Go away!'

'Archie, come out. I warned you not to go near the basement.'

'I'm not coming out until Mum and Dad get here.' Archie stuffed his things in his bag. He paced up and down, up and down. He couldn't wait until his parents arrived.

Knock. Knock. Knock.

'I'm calling the police when I get out of here!' called Archie. 'Go away.'

'Archie, it's Mum. Open the door.'

Archie dragged the furniture from the door, then flung it open. 'Aunt Ruth has a man-eating plant in the basement. It ate Uncle Jock and I was next!'

'Archie, Aunt Ruth told us everything. I know the plant looks scary but I'm sure it's not a man-eater. There's no such thing. I should have known you'd turn this visit into some kind of disaster.'

'How can you say that? She grew a monster! And nobody knows where Uncle Jock is? Aren't you worried about him?'

Archie ran out the door, down the passage, past his father and jumped into the car.

He locked the doors. Archie wasn't coming out of that car for anybody.

Suddenly an old ute came flying along the road and pulled up in a cloud of dust. The driver got out. He wore a fishing hat, vest and waterproof pants. In the back of the ute were fishing rods, tackle boxes and an esky.

'Uncle Jock?'

chapter fourteen

'Uncle Jock!' yelled Archie, springing from the car.

'It's me, alright. Wish I'd known you were here, Archie. You could've come fishing with me. Best trout I've ever caught. And they taste a whole lot better than you-know-who's stew,' he said with a wink.

'So you didn't get eaten by Aunt Ruth's plant!'

'Hoh! No I didn't get eaten. You poor kid. I told Ruth to get rid of that thing. She's got some wild idea that she and Cronk are going to make history.' He shrugged. 'Who knows? Maybe they will. But have you seen that thing? It's not a pretty sight.'

Archie felt so relieved. He looked around to see his parents, Aunt Ruth and Bob standing there. 'It's Uncle Jock. He's alive. He didn't get eaten!'

None of them looked happy with Archie. None of them at all.

Aunt Ruth plonked a large pot of tea on the table and a plate of her famous tomato cake. 'Hungry, everyone?'

Archie sat in-between his parents and grimaced at the strange red cake, while Aunt Ruth told everyone about the happenings of the last two days. First she told them about the experiment. How Roxanne grew into a gigantic plant. How Jock didn't like Roxanne, so she put her in the basement. How it was a scientific miracle and would be a world first. How Mr Cronk wanted to be famous too and helped her build the greenhouse. And how she tried to keep it a secret from Archie in case he freaked out, then told everyone.

'You nearly scared me to death with all that creeping around,' complained Archie.

'Archie, a lot of this has been your own doing,' said Mum. 'You and these ridiculous ideas. How many times did Aunt Ruth tell you to stay away from the basement?'

'I couldn't help it. I kept hearing weird noises. And Uncle Jock was missing.'

'S'pose I should've told Ruth where I was going,' chuckled Uncle Jock. 'She's always glad to get rid of me though, so I didn't bother.'

'Even Bob didn't like Roxanne. I thought she ate his leg,' said Archie.

'Nope. It was a croc, alright,' said Uncle Jock. 'I was there and it wasn't a pretty sight.'

'Well, I still want to know if Aunt Ruth sent any poisonous herbs to Cecil,' said Archie.

'Don't be ridiculous,' snapped Aunt Ruth. 'I wouldn't waste the postage. Whatever Cecil ate was something from one of his forest expeditions. He was always eating things he knew nothing about. Stupid.'

'There's no lungwort in that cake, is there?' Archie was feeling hungry.

'No!' said Aunt Ruth with a scowl.

'Good.' Archie lifted the cake to his mouth …

'But I thought I'd add some devil's beard,' she chuckled.

'Here, Bob, catch.' Archie threw the tomato

cake but Bob turned and ran out the door.

When the cake hit the floor, Aunt Ruth just shook her head. She shuffled outside, then brought something back. 'This is for you.' She plonked a potted seedling on the table in front of Archie. 'Your very own little herb. It's a new one that I've just cultivated. I call it Ruth Reticulata. Look after it, won't you, Archie?'

Archie stared at the plant. Then he decided it was his turn to give something to Aunt Ruth. He got up and gave her a big kiss on the cheek. *Mwah.* She turned a soft shade of pink.

Maybe Aunt Ruth wasn't so bad after all. Maybe it was just her cooking that was horrible. And maybe, he might even come back for another visit ... but not too soon.

meet kaye baillie

Kaye Baillie writes picture books, short stories and chapter books and sometimes dabbles with poetry. She has two published books in the educational market, *Diving at the Pool* and *Train Music* (Cengage Learning). *Archie Appleby* is Kaye's first chapter book with Wombat Books.

Kaye enjoys attending conferences and events relating to children's writing. When she is not scribbling down ideas for new stories she can be found at the library, walking her dog on the beach, eating cake, or trying to keep up with her two teenage daughters.

meet
krista brennan

Krista is a freelance illustrator, fine artist, art teacher and stained glass artist who lives in Sydney, Australia with her partner and mischievous cat. She primarily uses traditional methods for her art, including watercolour, ink and oils. Krista's art has been featured in books, card games, exhibitions and competitions, but she enjoys using her pictures to tell stories most of all.